SUGAR AND SPICE
The Pickpockets

Home Farm Twins

Sugar and Spice
The Pickpockets

Jenny Oldfield

Illustrated by Kate Aldous

*Hodder
Children's
Books*

a division of Hodder Headline plc

A Catalogue record for this book is available from the British Library

ISBN 0 340 69986 8

Typeset by Hewer Text Ltd, Edinburgh
Printed and bound in Great Britain by
Cox & Wyman Ltd, Reading, Berks

Hodder Children's Books
a division of Hodder Headline plc
338 Euston Road
London NW1 3BH

One

'Lambs!' Helen Moore suggested as she and her twin sister, Hannah, walked down Doveton High Street with their dog, Speckle.

'It's the wrong time of year,' Hannah pointed out. 'How about whooper swans?'

'They fly south for the winter.' It was late October and Helen had already seen the huge, graceful birds rise from the lake and head for warmer waters.

The twins needed an animal topic for their school science project. They had five days to choose the animal and complete the work, in time for Doveton Junior School's open evening the following Wednesday.

'Dogs?' Hannah suggested. They could take wonderful photographs of Speckle out on the fell.

Helen wrinkled her nose. 'Everyone will do dogs.'

'Or sheep,' Hannah said. Sheep were the lifeblood of the Lake District, where they lived. The bad-tempered, stubborn yet wonderful animals dotted the steep hillsides wherever they looked.

'We need something different,' Helen insisted.

'Now then, you two.' John Fox, the sheep farmer from Lakeside Farm, greeted them on the step of Luke Martin's village shop. John whistled for his dog, Ben, to jump into the back of the Land Rover and wait. 'Why so glum?' he asked the twins.

'We have to think of a subject for our school project,' Hannah explained. Then she brightened. Maybe the farmer could help! 'It must be an animal, but we love them all, so we can't decide which one.'

'Sheep.' John Fox's answer came quick as a flash.

'We already thought of that.' Helen told Speckle to sit, then gazed absent-mindedly at Luke's window. Jars of sweets stood alongside newspapers and boxes of fireworks.

'Did I ever tell you about a pet lamb of mine?' Mr

Fox launched into a tale that held Hannah in the shop doorway. Inside, she could hear the shopkeeper teaching his nephew, Sam Lawson, the prices of items on the neat shelves.

'Cheddar cheese has just gone up by three pence a kilo,' Luke said. 'I cut a piece to the size the customer wants, weigh it and price it like this. OK?'

'. . . I called this lamb Bruiser. A more swaggering, bullying sort of beast you could never wish to meet,' the farmer continued.

Hannah stared in surprise. To her, lambs were sweet, fluffy white creatures that skipped across spring meadows.

'By the time this lamb reached eighteen months, he weighed in at ninety pounds,' Mr Fox declared. 'He scared my dogs, stole biscuits from the table and attacked any stranger who came near!'

'Wow!' Hannah's mouth fell open. Perhaps they *should* choose Bruiser as their science topic. 'Could we come and see him?'

The farmer shook his head. 'Too late; Bruiser's gone. This was years ago.'

'What happened to him?' A fascinated Hannah made room for Helen to slip inside the shop.

'Died from over-eating.' Mr Fox kept a straight face. 'He got at a corn bin and ate until he burst!'

Hannah gulped and let the farmer go on his way. Ben wagged his tail at her from inside the car. She waved back, took a glance at the white doves perched on Luke's dovecote, then followed Helen into the shop.

'Of course, a squirrel's tail is the most amazing thing!' Luke Martin had moved on from the subject of cheese. His nephew, Sam, frowned at Helen from the doorway of the back room.

'It helps them to balance,' Helen agreed. 'That's why it's so long and bushy.'

'Exactly!' Luke realised he had found a willing audience in Helen and Hannah. He stopped stocking the shelves and came to the front of the counter. 'Squirrels are brilliantly designed,' he said eagerly. 'Their bones are light, so they weigh hardly anything and can jump a long way. Their claws are curved so they can grip when they land . . .'

'Uncle Luke!' Sam cut in. 'Where shall I put these bags of flour?'

'What? Oh, carry them upstairs for now, Sam. That's a good lad. As I was saying, squirrels can reach speeds on the ground of eighteen miles per hour!' Luke Martin's brown eyes sparkled in his round, smiling face.

'Who started him on the subject?' Hannah whispered to Helen. The shopkeeper was spouting more squirrel information.

'. . . Belonging to the family *Sciuridae*, to give them their proper scientific name. The American grey squirrel has a longer, larger head than the native red squirrel . . .' Luke rattled off the facts.

'Not me!' Helen muttered back to Hannah. 'He was already giving Sam a lecture on them when I came in!'

'. . . Of course, it's not true that the grey squirrel drove the red squirrel out of its natural habitat, as people like to think. No, the real reason for the decline of the red squirrel was the destruction of the conifer forests. The red squirrel lives on pine cones. No pine trees: no red squirrel! Simple as that!'

An idea crept into Hannah's head. She cupped her hand round her mouth and whispered again, just as Sam Lawson picked up the box of flour-bags to carry it upstairs. 'Helen, what about squirrels?'

'For our topic!' Helen nodded and spoke loudly. 'Squirrels: yes!' Pretty, dark eyed, bushy-tailed acro-

bats. Furry and silky, sleek and graceful. What could be better?

'Oh no you don't!' Sam hissed. 'Squirrels are *my* topic!'

'So?' Helen didn't see why she and Hannah shouldn't choose the same animal as Sam.

'So, it's not fair!' The boy from their class sulked and pulled a face. 'I thought of it first! That's why I asked Uncle Luke!'

'Oh come on, Sam!' Luke Martin overheard and stepped in to prevent a row. 'What's the problem? The twins can do squirrels too!'

So Sam glowered and stamped off upstairs. 'Not fair,' he grumbled when he thought he was out of earshot. 'You two are just copycats! Anyway, my project will be better than yours, just you wait!'

Helen shrugged it off. 'How come you know so much about squirrels?' she asked Luke.

'I've been reading up about them,' he explained. 'You know, one really fascinating thing is that . . .'

'Stop!' Hannah grinned and put up both hands. 'Why?'

'Why?' Helen repeated. 'Why did you want to find out all about them?'

'Ah!' His smile broadened behind his neat beard. He beckoned and let them into a proud secret. 'Because I have a squirrel in my loft!'

'To go with the doves in your dovecote!' Hannah grinned. The white birds fluttered and flew off as she, Helen and Luke stood looking up at the roof. Speckle, who had been waiting patiently by the door, came to join them.

Luke had taken them outside the shop to show them how the squirrel visitor came and went. He pointed to the eaves of the old stone building. Ivy grew up the wall and reached the top of the gable. 'There's a small hole between the gutter and the roof,' he explained. 'I'm sure that's the way the squirrel gets into the loft.'

'Does it jump from those trees?' Helen peered into the tall beech trees behind the shop, hoping for a glimpse of the grey squirrel. The leaves had turned golden brown and were dropping gently on to the roof and pavement.

'Not in one hop,' Luke explained. 'I've seen it jump from the lowest branch on to the dovecote, and then on to the roof.'

Just then, the bell fixed to Luke's shop door rang and another customer went in. He left Hannah and Helen to study the squirrel's route alone.

They were guessing the distance between the lowest branch and the white dovecote when a shower of brown leaves fell from the beech tree.

'What was that?' Hannah cried. She craned her neck to look up into the high branches.

Speckle wagged his tail and yapped.

Helen caught sight of a tail whisking down the trunk. Then it vanished round the far side. 'Squirrel!' she whispered.

They waited. More leaves showered to the ground. A round face peered round the tree trunk, little hands reached out on to a branch. The squirrel gathered courage and stepped back into view.

'*Swee-eet*!' Hannah sighed.

The squirrel sat on the branch, then reared on to its hind legs. It clutched at a leaf and held it tight between its front paws. Jerkily, one hop at a time, it ventured out along the branch, then waited.

'Here comes another!' Helen spotted a second squirrel run quickly down the trunk. Its bushy tail was curled up over its head, its ears were pricked.

'*Two* squirrels!' Helen wanted to rush and tell Luke the good news. Not one, but two squirrels in his loft.

But the tiny creatures seemed to like the fact that they had an audience. They grew bolder, darting along the branch, then swinging to a lower one. The slender branch dipped and swung under their weight, but they clung on tight, then leaped again.

'Oh!' Hannah held her breath.

'It's OK. They're showing off!' Helen grinned.

The squirrels tumbled like acrobats from branch to branch, using their tails as rudders.

'Did you know that squirrels can swim?' Luke popped his head out of the door as his customer left the shop.

'Er, no. Luke; did you know you've got a *pair* of them in your loft?' Hannah pointed to the swaying branch. The two squirrels peered down with their big dark eyes.

He came out grinning from ear to ear. 'You're right! The happy couple must be building a nest in there!'

'Can we give them names?' Helen begged.

'Sugar and Spice because they're so *swee-eet*!' Hannah cried.

'Sugar and Spice it is,' Luke agreed.

'Stupid names!' Sam Lawson muttered as he came out of the shop and got on to his bike. He rode off with a scowl.

'Bye, Sam. See you later,' Luke called. He stared up at the squirrels. 'They seem quite tame.'

'And cheeky!' Helen grinned as the first squirrel took a flying leap from the branch to the dovecote roof. A startled dove popped its head out of the door, then flew off.

'They're youngsters by the look of it,' Luke decided. 'This is probably their first autumn, so they'll be busy building a drey together.'

'A nest? In your loft?' Hannah quizzed him. 'Will they store food in there?'

He nodded. 'Nuts and roots; stuff like that. Flower bulbs, insects; they'll eat just about anything.'

Helen made a mental note. These facts were going to be useful for their science project.

'Blackberries?' Hannah asked. She saw now where the squirrels were heading. There was an overgrown bramble hedge behind the wall that ran alongside the pavement. Juicy ripe fruit still hung from the thorny branches.

They watched the squirrels perch on the dovecote roof and sit perfectly still.

'Make up your minds!' Helen urged.

'We won't hurt you!' Hannah promised.

The squirrels' tails twitched, their dark eyes glittered.

Then they made a final, perfect leap. They were on the wall, scrambling along, snatching at the berries and stuffing them into their mouths before Speckle had a chance to bark or the twins had time to follow their movement.

'Blackberries for pudding!' Helen grinned.

The squirrels' dainty paws picked and stuffed. They twitched their whiskers and whisked their tails.

Grrr . . . rragh! A furry cream-coloured whirlwind flew down the main street, snarling as it came.

Speckle whirled round and stood fast. The twins gasped as the squirrels froze in mid-bite.

'Puppy!' A voice yelled after the growling, bad-tempered attacker.

'Mr Winter!' Luke groaned at the rude disruption of the squirrels' dessert.

The cairn terrier flung himself at the wall, leaping up, barking and yapping.

The squirrels blinked, turned and ran. They were up on the dovecote, leaping for the tree. Within seconds, after a final whisk of their bushy tails, they were gone.

Two

'Keep those creatures away from my dog! Put Speckle on a lead!' Cecil Winter, ex-headteacher of Doveton Junior, fired off commands. He rolled down the main street like a tank going into battle.

'Uh-oh!' Hannah sighed. She knew they were in for a telling-off from the short-tempered old man.

Helen glanced at Speckle. Their dog was sitting, good as gold. He looked up at her, head to one side, as if to say, 'Here comes trouble!'

Mr Winter rumbled towards them, blue blazer smartly buttoned, trousers pressed, grey moustache trimmed. 'Puppy!' He rapped out the dog's name, struggling to be heard above the terrier's raucous bark.

'It's OK, Mr Winter.' Helen stepped boldly across his path. 'The squirrels have gone. Anyway, they wouldn't do Puppy any harm.'

'Not do any harm?' he repeated, staring at her from under his bushy eyebrows. He'd finally ground to a halt outside the shop.

Speckle beat a hasty retreat under the nearby bench.

'Well, no.' Helen felt herself go hot. She flicked back her heavy fringe and swallowed hard. 'Puppy's bigger than they are. They're probably frightened of him!'

'Frightened of Puppy?' the old man echoed incredulously.

The terrier barked and leaped up at the wall long after the squirrels had disappeared up the tree.

'Dogs are one of the grey squirrel's main enemies,' Luke confirmed. 'Along with foxes, cats, eagles, hawks, owls . . .'

'Yes, yes.' Mr Winter sniffed and twitched his moustache. 'That's all very well. But Puppy is a timid dog. He suffers with his nerves.'

Puppy yapped and jumped up.

Hannah stepped forward and softly called his name. 'Here, Puppy. Come here, that's a good boy!' 'Puppy' wasn't a puppy at all, but a six-year-old bundle of snappy cream fur. His black nose came snuffling against her outstretched hand, his small, beady eyes peered out from behind a shaggy fringe.

'Hmph!' Mr Winter blew down his nose, then cleared his throat. 'The fact remains, we don't want the village to be overrun with squirrels this autumn.'

'Why not?' Helen asked.

'Why not? Because they're pests; that's why not!'

'Pests?' It was Hannah's turn to echo.

'Yes. Ask any keen gardener if he wants a squirrel in his garden, and you'll find the answer is a resounding no. Squirrels cause serious timber damage. They strip bark from trees, they eat fruit from bushes . . . need I go on?' The old teacher hammered his point home.

'But they're sweet,' Hannah protested.

Helen jabbed her with her elbow. Wrong thing to say!

'Sweet?' Mr Winter nearly exploded. He went red to the top of his shiny bald head.

Under the bench, Speckle lowered his chin to the ground and whined.

Luke stepped in to save the twins. 'Is there anything you need from the shop before I close for the day?' he asked the fuming ex-teacher.

'Nothing, thank you!' Mr Winter turned on his heel and squared his shoulders. 'Come along, Puppy!'

'Go home!' Hannah stooped and gave the terrier a gentle shove.

Puppy wagged his short, pointed tail and lolled his pink tongue.

'Puppy!' came the sharp command once more. Mr Winter was striding up the street, head up, shoulders back.

'Go!' Hannah insisted.

Yap-yap! Yap-yap! Puppy bounded off after his owner on his short little legs.

Luke shrugged and grinned. 'What about you? Is there anything you'd like from the shop?'

'No, thanks.' Helen breathed a sigh of relief.

'But would it be OK if we looked in your loft?' Hannah put in a quick request. 'Speckle could wait outside for us. He won't make a fuss.'

'We wouldn't disturb the squirrels,' Helen promised. 'We only want to look at where they're build-ing their nest.'

'Drey,' Luke corrected. 'I take it that you've definitely decided on squirrels for your school pro-ject?'

'Yes!' Helen and Hannah chorused.

'Well, go ahead and take a look.' He told Speckle to wait, then invited the twins inside and through to the back of the shop. The storeroom overflowed with boxes and bulky packets. A narrow, dark flight of stairs led off to one side. Luke pointed the way. 'Up the stairs, along the landing. There's a small door at the end. That's the way into the loft. Watch your head as you go in!'

So Hannah and Helen squeezed past a cardboard box full of tinned soup, following the shopkeeper's directions.

The old stairs creaked as they went up. Empty plastic crates were stacked against the landing wall, and the door to the loft was blocked by the box of flour that Sam had carried up earlier.

'Anyone would think Sam didn't want us to get in here!' Hannah grumbled. She pulled the heavy box clear of the door.

'Shh!' Helen was ready to lift the latch. She opened the door to the musty loft.

'I can't see a thing!' Hannah hissed, stooping to go in. She had to wait until her eyes got used to the dark.

Then she could make out a low, sloping roof supported by cobwebby beams. There was an old, dusty trunk in one corner, a broken chair, a cracked mirror leaning against the wall. Above their heads, they heard doves coo and call from the roof.

'Creepy!' Helen whispered. She saw her own dim reflection in the mirror, cut in two and distorted by the crack. 'I look like I've got four eyes!'

'What exactly are we looking for?' Hannah wanted to know. 'What does a squirrels' drey look like?'

'I suppose it's a kind of twiggy thing. Like a big bird's nest.' Helen peered into the far corners. There were packing-cases in one, an old roller-blind that must have once hung at the front of the shop in another.

'Like that?' Hannah pointed to an untidy bundle of sticks, perched on one of the tea-chest packing-cases. It was roughly round and the size of a football.

Helen nodded. 'That must be it!' It was the first squirrels' drey she'd ever seen, but there was no mistaking the frame of twigs lined with moss and leaves.

'Maybe Sugar and Spice aren't very good at nest building yet!' Hannah grinned. 'Luke said it was probably their first winter together.'

'At least they chose somewhere warm.' Helen pointed to a thick metal water-pipe that ran alongside the packing-case. 'That's for hot water.'

'Can you see where they come in?' Hannah wanted to investigate, but the floor of the loft was cluttered, and she couldn't tread safely in the dark.

In any case, Helen suddenly grabbed her arm. 'Did you hear that?' she whispered.

Hannah listened to the scratching, scrabbling sounds on the roof above their heads. At first she thought it was more doves landing and strutting along the ridge. But these feet made a pattering, scurrying noise.

'It's them! They're on their way to the drey!' Helen hissed. She ducked behind the wooden chest and dragged Hannah with her.

Chuck-chuck-char! One of the squirrels scrabbled down the roof, chattering as he came.

Wruhh-wruhh! The other gave a softer, rolling call.

'Look!' Hannah pointed to a crack of light between the roof and a stout beam. There was a tiny hole in the angle there, just large enough for a squirrel to squeeze through.

A small, furry, grey face appeared. Huge eyes gleamed.

Then the squirrel pushed its whole body through the gap. It clung upside down to the broad beam, its bushy tail hanging, its sharp claws digging into the wood.

'That's Spice,' Hannah decided. He was the squirrel with more browny-red fur on his face and belly.

'Here comes Sugar,' Helen murmured.

The female was smaller, and her tail had a definite white fringe. Her coat was silvery grey.

The two squirrels scrambled along the underside of the beam, then dropped silently to the floor. They reared on to their hind legs, tails flat, ears erect, sniffing the musty air.

Wrruhh! Sugar moaned softly.

Spice whisked his tail and set off for the drey. He ran in a zigzag across the cluttered floor, stopping every now and then to listen. *Char-char-chuck!* He turned to Sugar and ordered her to follow.

The smaller squirrel put on a sudden spurt. She overtook Spice and leaped for the drey, scrambling up the tea chest and vanishing in a flash.

Chuck! Spice took one last look round and went in after her.

'Weren't they brilliant?' Hannah had crept out of the loft once she was sure that Sugar and Spice had settled into the drey.

'I suppose they must be asleep for the night,' Helen sighed. They'd waited for what seemed like an age for the squirrels to reappear, but without any luck. She closed the door to the loft, then leaned against it.

'Do you think Luke will let us come back to take photos?' Hannah was planning ahead. Their dad, David Moore, earned his living as a photographer. They could borrow one of his cameras, use his dark-room in the attic at Home Farm to develop the film and print the pictures for the display at school.

'Miss Wesley said the more pictures we could find of our animals the better mark we'd get for the project,' Helen said. 'If we ask Luke, I'm sure he'll say yes!'

'We'll have to get a move on,' Hannah reminded her. 'Today's Saturday. We've only got until next Wednesday.'

She was all for collecting Speckle and heading straight home to begin work. But, as she set off along the landing, something crackled underfoot and she looked down.

'What is it?' In her rush, Helen cannoned into the back of her.

'Chocolate wrappers,' Hannah mumbled. A piece of melted chocolate had stuck one wrapper to her shoe. 'What are they doing here?'

Helen bent to investigate. The wrappers were chewed and mangled by sharp teeth. 'Uh-oh!' As she picked one up, she began to put two and two together.

'Some kind of animal's been at these!' Hannah frowned as she scraped the wrapper off her sole. Her eyes widened. 'Helen, you don't think . . . !'

Helen stared back at the closed door. She nodded. 'Yes, I do think . . . !'

'That Sugar and Spice have . . . ?'

'Been downstairs and raided Luke's shop?' Helen finished the sentence. 'Looks like it!' She pictured the cheeky squirrels finding their way under the door, scuttling across the landing and down the stairs in the dead of night. They would patter across the storeroom floor, their noses would twitch at all the wonderful scents coming from behind Luke's counters . . . The rest didn't take much imagination.

Hannah collected bits of silver paper and coloured wrappers and screwed them into a ball. 'Don't say anything about this!' she said, hurriedly shoving the wrappers into her pocket.

'Hadn't we better mention it to Luke?' Helen asked.

She ran after Hannah, who went downstairs two at a time.

'There's no point making a fuss.' Hannah was already through the storeroom and saying thank you to the shopkeeper. 'Please can we come back tomorrow and take some photos?'

'Come whenever you like.' He smiled pleasantly as he tidied away the cheeses. 'Take as many photos as you like. Ask me any questions about squirrels and I'll try to give you the right answers!'

'Thanks!' Helen grinned back at him, forgetting all about the sweet wrappers.

They heard a car draw up outside the shop, recognised Sam Lawson's straw-coloured hair through the window.

'That must be my sister, Carrie, and Sam again. I invited them for tea.' Luke went to the door. As he said goodbye to the twins, he greeted the new arrivals.

'And Ollie!' Carrie Lawson kissed her brother on the cheek. She was a young, pretty woman with light-brown wavy hair. 'I hope you don't mind us bringing the puppy!'

A black, brown and white scrap of energy on four

legs bounded across the pavement. Big brown ears flopped, white paws jumped up. Ollie was a beagle pup, about four months old, and a bundle of unstoppable motion.

From under the bench Speckle wagged his tail. Helen and Hannah stooped to pet the pup, enjoying the feel of his rough pink tongue on their hands and arms.

'We didn't want to leave him behind at Crackpot Farm,' Carrie explained.

She ignored the fact that Sam was scowling at the twins as he pushed his way through the door.

'Hi, Sam!' Hannah tried to make friends.

'How would you fancy sharing photos for the project?' Helen asked.

It was no good. Sam Lawson was still mad at them for muscling in on his idea.

His mother bent to scoop the puppy into her arms. As she disappeared inside the house with Sam and Luke, the twins heard her excuses for bringing the pup.

'. . . Ollie hates being in the house by himself. I know he chewed your slippers and tried to eat your furniture the last time he came. But do you think you could *possibly* stand another visit?'

Three

'They hide their food-stores in hollow trees,' Hannah told Helen across the kitchen table. She read out the latest squirrel fact from a wildlife book belonging to David Moore.

It was Sunday morning, and the twins had gone squirrel-mad. Helen was writing out a list of what they ate: berries, pollen, roots, bulbs, eggs, insects . . . 'Chocolate!' she whispered to herself with a grin.

'Don't write that down!' Hannah hissed. Her dad had just given them a curious look. She cleared her throat and read on: ' "A squirrel holds its food in its forefeet. It can eat between one hundred and one hundred and fifty pine cones per day." '

'*Per day!*' Helen struggled to write it all down. Her handwriting scrawled across the page. 'This is only rough,' she explained to her dad. 'We'll type it up on the school computer tomorrow.'

'It looks as if a spider crawled across the page.' David Moore leaned over her shoulder. 'You spell "pollen" with a double-l.'

'That *is* a double-l!' Helen protested. 'Anyway, if "pollen" has a double-l, why doesn't "Helen"?'

'Because . . .' David Moore was about to launch into a long explanation when the phone rang and he went into the hall to answer it.

'Saved by the bell!' Hannah sighed. 'Spelt with a double l! Here, Helen, write this next bit down . . .'

There were facts about how a squirrel nibbled a pine cone and split a beech-nut shell, how it stripped bark from a tree in long, spiral twists . . .

'Hannah – Helen, can one of you come to the phone for a second?' David Moore popped his head around the door. 'It's Mr Winter. He wants to ask you a question about Puppy.'

'*Aagh!*' Helen pretended to scream. She could have sworn that Speckle, who lay quietly in his basket by the warm stove, cringed at the sound of Puppy's name. 'You go!' she mouthed at Hannah. 'I have to look upstairs for the camera Dad said we could borrow!'

Hannah went into the hall and gingerly took the phone from her dad.

'Helen, this is Cecil Winter here . . . !' The old man rattled off his words like machine-gun bullets.

'This is Hannah speaking, Mr Winter.' She dived in with the correction.

'Helen – Hannah, it doesn't matter which. You were both there when those two squirrels attacked Puppy outside Luke Martin's shop yesterday afternoon, weren't you?'

Hannah was startled. 'I . . . we . . .'

'Good, well I'd like you to tell me exactly what happened before I arrived on the scene!'

'I'm not sure what you mean. All we saw was Sugar and Spice coming down the beech tree to nibble at some blackberries behind the wall, and . . .'

'Sugar and Spice?' Mr Winter repeated in a puzzled voice.

'Sorry, I mean the pair of squirrels from Luke's loft . . .'

There was a long silence. But if Hannah hoped that the ex-headteacher had run out of ammunition, she was mistaken. The pause was only for reloading, then *rattle-rattle-rattle* came the quick-fire questions.

'So you mean to say that the squirrels have actually invaded the village shop? Why didn't Luke Martin tell me this when I phoned him earlier this morning? Have they built their drey inside the building? Whereabouts is it? Did you say it was in the loft? Does Luke store food for the shop up there?'

Hannah held the phone away from her ear. She could hear Puppy barking and yapping in the background as Mr Winter fired away.

'Are you still there?' the cross voice barked.

'Yes, I'm here. I'm sorry, Mr Winter, I've forgotten what you wanted to know.' She raised her eyebrows at Helen, who came downstairs with the camera.

'What happened outside the shop yesterday? That was my original question, though of course I am most concerned to hear you say that the squirrels are anywhere near foodstuff that's offered for sale to the general public.'

'We didn't see much.' Hannah jumped in as quickly as she could. She could picture the old man's moustache quivering with indignation. His face would be beetroot red. 'The squirrels were on the wall. Puppy came barking along the street. The squirrels ran away.'

'Is that all?' Mr Winter obviously didn't believe her. 'Are you sure that you didn't see the vicious little things attacking poor Puppy?'

'No, honestly!' Hannah stuck up for Sugar and Spice. 'The squirrels didn't do anything to Puppy! If anything, *they* were frightened by *him*!'

'*Harrumph!*' Mr Winter snorted. 'So how do you explain the scratch on Puppy's nose?'

'What kind of scratch?' Hannah pressed the phone closer to her ear and frowned.

'A deep, savage scratch across the bridge of his nose. Definitely made by a small, sharp claw. Had to bathe it with disinfectant when I got the poor chap home. Took it well, of course. Never one to make a fuss!'

In the background, the cairn terrier yapped and whined.

'But Sugar and . . . the squirrels didn't go near Puppy, Mr Winter!'

Helen stood nearby, clutching the camera and nodding hard. She'd picked up the accusations that the ex-teacher was flinging at Luke's squirrels.

'Helen says the same as me,' Hannah added.

'Hah! I might have known you two girls would close ranks with Luke Martin!'

By now Mr Winter was hardly pausing to listen. His voice rose as he returned to the attack. 'You animal lovers are all the same. No notion of the harm that vermin such as squirrels can do!'

Hannah held the phone at arm's length again. Mr Winter was going on and on. All she could do was stand quietly and let him have his say.

'You come from the town, where people know nothing about the reality of living in the country.' He *psshawed* and *harrumphed*. 'Let me remind you, my girl, that you and your twin sister are wearing rose-coloured spectacles!

'Never!' he insisted, shouting down the phone at full volume; 'Never forget that squirrels are merely rats with bushy tails!'

'Mr Winter's upset about Puppy, that's all.' Luke greeted Helen and Hannah with a cheerful smile. He'd said yes when they'd rung him to ask if they could take pictures of Sugar and Spice, and told them to come straight down.

The village shop was open for business, even though it was a Sunday. Golden-brown leaves fluttered on to the pavement from the beech trees above, so the shopkeeper was out with his broom, clearing the path. 'If I were you, I wouldn't give it a second thought. Just give him time to cool down, and he'll forget all about the squirrels in my loft!'

Hannah had told Luke about Mr Winter's accusations.

'What's he going to do? He can't very well have the squirrels dragged before a judge, accused of attacking his dog, can he?' Luke grinned again. He mimed the judge passing sentence with a serious face and a gruff voice: ' "Grievous bodily harm. Guilty. Six months in prison!" '

Helen giggled. 'The thing is, Sugar and Spice didn't even *touch* Puppy!' she protested. 'He must have cut his nose on the bramble bush!' She stooped to pick up some beech nuts in their spiky cups and showed them to Hannah. 'We could make these part of our display.'

'A whole section on what squirrels eat?' Hannah

nodded. She picked up more nuts and put them carefully in her pocket. Her fingertips touched the screwed-up silver paper from the chocolate wrappers that they'd found on Luke's landing the day before. She jerked her fingers out of her pocket and hummed noisily.

But as they went upstairs with their camera, she felt hot and guilty. 'Maybe we should tell Luke about the chocolate after all,' she whispered to Helen.

'No way!' Helen had reached the landing and was taking the camera out of its case. 'Sugar and Spice are in enough trouble with Mr Winter as it is. We don't want to go spreading more rumours about them that might not even be true!'

'Luke won't tell anyone.' Hannah frowned down at the floor. She waited for Helen to set the flash on the camera, ready to creep through the low door into the dark loft.

The landing was still stacked with cardboard boxes. The door at the far end was tightly closed. But there on the floor was more evidence that the cheeky squirrels had been out on another raid. Hannah gasped and pointed. 'Helen!' she whispered.

As Hannah spoke, Helen's right foot trod on a sticky

spot on the floor. She knew what it was without having to look. 'Chocolate?'

Hannah nodded.

'But the loft door's still shut!' Helen didn't want to believe the evidence squashed on the sole of her shoe.

'Sugar and Spice must be able to squeeze under that tiny gap!' Hannah pointed again; this time to a narrow space between the door and the floor.

'It's too small!' Helen argued.

'How are you getting on?' Luke called from the store-room below. His voice made them jump guiltily.

'Fine!' Helen pulled herself together and tried the door latch.

'If you're lucky, you might find the squirrels are active around now.'

As Luke came halfway up the stairs, Helen quickly scraped the squashed chocolate off her shoe. She stuck it straight into her pocket.

'I hear them moving about in the loft first thing in the morning for a couple of hours, then again just before dusk.' Luke was doing his best to be helpful. He came up to the landing to shift a box out of their way. 'We put the clocks back last night, so it'll be dusk pretty soon. Sugar and Spice should be out and about looking for their supper!'

'Thanks!' Helen said faintly. She felt the chocolate melt inside her pocket. 'It looks like they already found it!' she muttered quietly to Hannah as Luke carried the box downstairs.

'You don't mind if I carry on tidying up, do you?' Luke called up as he reached the storeroom with the box.

'No, that's fine!' Helen heaved a sigh of relief.

'Only, I'm still trying to recover from Sam and Carrie's visit with Ollie last night. Honestly, that little dog is a real handful! He looks as if butter wouldn't melt in his mouth, but you have to have eyes in the back of your head if you want to keep him out of trouble!' Luke's good-natured grumbling faded as he moved from room to room.

'Ready?' Hannah's urge to confess about the squirrels' love of chocolate had faded. Now she just wanted to get on with taking the photographs.

So they crept into the loft and took up position.

'You might have to wait a long time,' their dad had warned them when he dropped them off at the shop. 'We wildlife photographers need the patience of a saint!' He'd winked and driven off to collect their mum from the Curlew Cafe which she ran in Nesfield. 'I'll pick you up on the way back,' he'd promised.

Fifteen minutes went by in dark silence. Helen's legs began to ache from crouching in one position behind a packing case. Twice Hannah thought she heard movements from inside the squirrels' untidy drey.

'Sorry, false alarm!' she breathed each time.

Then, just when they thought that Luke's prediction about seeing the squirrels had been wrong, they did hear the telltale sounds of sharp claws rattling over the stone roof above their heads. The creatures ran in short bursts, then paused, then ran again. Helen and Hannah fixed their gaze on the tiny crack of light in the eaves where they knew the squirrels would enter.

And sure enough, a face appeared. It stared into the loft, its long whiskers and huge eyes only just visible. Then Spice popped the whole of his head through the gap and eased his forelegs on to the broad wooden beam. Soon, his lithe grey body and great bushy tail followed.

Helen raised the camera and aimed at the squirrel.

'Wait until Sugar gets in the shot!' Hannah whispered. They needed both squirrels in the photograph, to show that Sugar and Spice were a pair.

The smaller female squirrel soon squeezed through the gap and flicked her tail. *Tuk-tuk-tuk*! she warned. She checked this way and that before she followed Spice along the underside of the beam.

Ignoring the more timid female, bold Spice scampered quickly ahead. He leaped in a fluid movement from his upside-down position on the beam to the top of the tea chest where the young squirrels built their drey. He twisted in midair and landed with a thump of his back feet on the hollow case. Then he sat on his hind legs, sniffing and twitching his whiskers.

Helen pointed the camera and waited. She knew she would only get one chance; once the bright light had flashed, Sugar and Spice would turn tail and vanish. The first shot had to be perfect.

Hannah saw Sugar leap through the air after Spice. For a few seconds, they both sat outside the drey, reared on their hind legs, front paws drooping. 'Now!' she hissed.

Click-flash! Helen pressed the button. She'd caught them looking in the direction of the camera, ears pricked, heads up. 'Perfect!' she breathed.

But all Hannah could see, when her eyes got over the sudden flash of bright light, was an empty space on top of the tea chest. The nest of leaves and twigs trembled and shook, but the squirrels were nowhere to be seen.

Four

'Now, remember; your science projects must be finished by the end of school tomorrow!' Miss Wesley announced.

It was Monday afternoon, and the whole class had been working on their animal topics all day.

Hannah had cleared away scissors and glue, while Helen finished printing off sheets about Sugar and Spice's drey. That evening their dad would help them to develop and print the roll of film that included the photo they'd taken in Luke's loft.

'You must bring everything to do with your project

to school tomorrow morning,' the teacher went on. 'We'll spend the day mounting your information and making a display for the entrance hall. I want your very best work, to impress visitors to the school's open evening.'

She walked up and down the aisles as pupils rushed to clear away before the bell went, but she stopped by Sam Lawson's desk. 'Fold your stuff neatly, Sam,' she said with a frown, watching him stuff sheets of paper into his bag. 'We won't be able to put it on the wall if it gets screwed up like that.'

'I don't care.' Sam zipped his bag shut and stared at the floor. 'It's useless anyway.'

Hannah paused to listen. Sam had been in a bad mood all day, hanging over his work, refusing to let anyone look. Now, as the bell for the end of school rang out and Miss Wesley dismissed the class, she sidled up to him.

'Do you want to join in with Helen and me on our project?' she said quietly. After all, to Sam it must look as if they'd muscled in on his idea.

He strode ahead. 'Nope.'

'We could share a display sheet,' she persisted, following him out of the door and across the playground. 'If we put all our stuff together, it would make a better project!'

Sam headed for the gate, where his mum, Carrie Lawson, waited with Ollie, the beagle pup. 'No!' He turned and rejected her offer once and for all. 'Look, I don't care about the stupid project. OK?'

Hannah stopped and sighed. She waited for Helen and watched Sam's puppy jump up and smother him in licks as he reached the gate. His mum got them both into the Land Rover, then drove off.

'Never mind. You tried.' Helen shrugged. 'Come on. I'm going to stop at the shop for some new felt-tip pens!' She wanted their project to look bold and colourful.

Hannah smiled. 'Any excuse!'

'For what?' Helen acted the innocent.

'For sneaking up to Luke's loft to find Sugar and Spice!' Hannah could read her sister's mind. She would be looking at felt-tips, waiting for her chance to ask the shopkeeper if they could nip up to his loft for another teenie-weenie glance.

'So?' Helen demanded.

'So!' Hannah grinned. 'Great idea. Let's go!'

They tramped through the banks of fallen leaves along the pavement, past the deserted cricket pavilion that overlooked the smooth pitch, until they came to a row of stone terraced houses with neat front gardens. A hairy cream face peered through one of the gates and yapped at them as they passed.

'Hello, Puppy!' Helen said, stopping to give the terrier a friendly pat. After all, a dog couldn't choose its owner. 'Where's this scratch on your nose, then?'

Hannah came and peered closely at Puppy's face. 'There!' She pointed to a small cut above his black nose that had already healed over.

'That's tiny!' Helen had expected to see an ugly chunk gouged out of the dog's face. She looked up at the house and saw that from behind his net curtain at the front-room window, Mr Winter twitched and glowered.

The twins moved quickly on. 'He told us it was deep and savage!' Hannah muttered. But when they spied the Lawsons' Land Rover outside Luke's shop, they soon forgot about Puppy's injury.

'Do you still want to go in?' Helen stopped under the beech trees and held back. It might be better to keep out of Sam Lawson's way until the animal projects were handed in and forgotten.

But, in any case, the Lawsons were already on their way out of the shop. Ollie bounded first through the door and came charging at the twins. His floppy ears flew, his stumpy tail wagged as he launched himself at Helen.

Carrie Lawson came running after the black, brown and white puppy. 'Get down, Ollie!' she scolded.

Helen caught hold of the wriggling pup. 'It's OK. He can probably smell Speckle on my clothes.'

'And chocolate biscuit crumbs in your lunch-box!' Hannah giggled as the puppy's tail wagged in Helen's face. He was snuffling eagerly at Helen's schoolbag.

Mrs Lawson seized Ollie. 'Naughty boy! You really are going to get into serious trouble one of these days!'

Helen laughed as he squirmed and struggled. She noticed that Sam had ignored them and was climbing into the Land Rover. Then, when Mrs Lawson had firm hold of Ollie, she too headed for the car and the twins went on into the shop.

' "Schoolgirl Attacked by Disorderly Beagle Pup!" '

Luke made up a newspaper headline as he grinned at Helen. ' "Ten-year-old twin, Helen Moore, is recovering from her frightening ordeal inside local shopkeeper Luke Martin's village premises!" '

'Phew!' Helen leaned against the counter.

'Ollie's not even supposed to come inside the shop,' Luke explained. 'But every time Carrie and Sam call, he seems to manage to sneak in somehow.'

'He's sweet.' Hannah defended the energetic beagle pup.

'And never does a thing he's told!' Luke grinned. He waited for Helen to draw breath. 'Now that you've survived the Ollie-attack, what can I do for you?'

But neither Helen nor Hannah had time to answer before the shop bell jangled and Mr Winter strode in.

'Right!' he barked, shooting looks to left and right. 'Where are they?'

Helen and Hannah glanced around the shop.

'Where are who?' Luke's face fell as he retreated behind the counter.

'You know perfectly well who! The squirrels; that's

who!' He fixed his angry gaze on the twins. 'That's why these two are here; to see this pair of tame ones that you keep. Yes, yes; I know that they even have names, so there's no point denying it!'

'Mr Winter . . .' Luke began. He leaned forward over the counter. 'You can see for yourself that there are no squirrels in the shop.

The ex-headteacher stomped here and there. He poked behind the newspaper stand, peered under the cheese counter, ran his eyes along the high shelves behind the counter. 'Where are you hiding them?' he demanded.

'Nowhere.' Luke struggled to stay calm. 'The squirrels aren't pets. They're wild animals.'

'They live in the loft.' Hannah gave Mr Winter the facts. 'They've made their winter nest, and they come and go through a gap in the roof.'

'That's right. There's no way they can get out of the loft and come downstairs!' Luke insisted.

Helen narrowed her eyes at Hannah and pursed her lips. *Don't tell him anything!*

'So you say!' The old man pushed his way behind the counter and peered into the storeroom. 'But since they attacked poor Puppy, I've been making some inquiries.'

'What kind of inquiries?' For the first time, Luke sounded worried.

'I've been asking the kind of questions that any right-minded, public-spirited person would want answers to. There are health worries here. Squirrels spread diseases. They must on no account come near food that's for sale!'

'Of course not!' Luke sprang to his own defence. 'I wouldn't dream of letting the squirrels stay in the loft if I thought there was any chance they would be able to get through the door and into the shop!'

Hannah swallowed hard. Was it finally time to own up about the chocolate wrappers on the landing? But if they did, what would happen to Sugar and Spice?

'The public health authority would come down on you like a ton of bricks if they found the slightest risk of these two squirrels spreading disease!' Mr Winter warned. 'I've spoken to the pest control office today. They made it quite plain to me that they'd be over here to deal with the situation straight away if I could give them any evidence that there was a problem!'

Helen gasped. She saw Luke grasp the edge of the counter. 'What does he mean exactly?' she whispered to Hannah.

'About the pest control people?' Hannah could only guess. But she dreaded what lay behind the sinister phrase 'deal with the situation'.

'Poison?' Helen muttered. The very word scared her.

'Traps!' Hannah closed her eyes and held her breath. Or both? A trap baited with poison. A cruel spring waiting to be triggered.

They stood helpless as Mr Winter continued on the warpath.

'Go ahead. Take a look,' Luke told him. He stepped

aside to show him upstairs to the loft. 'I'm telling you as plainly as I can that there's no risk attached to having the squirrels' nest up there. The loft door stays firmly shut twenty-four hours a day. There's absolutely no way that the squirrels could come through!'

Five

'That's a very good enlargement, girls!' David Moore stood back to admire the portrait of Sugar and Spice by their drey.

Hannah and Helen watched the big picture take shape in the dish of printing fluid. The two squirrels looked bright-eyed and eager, perched on their hind legs with their tails curved over their heads.

'I couldn't have taken a better one myself.' Their dad used tweezers to lift the photograph out of the dish and into a tank for fixing. 'So how come you're not over the moon about it?'

'We are,' Helen sighed. It was one of the best pictures she'd ever taken.

'It's perfect for our project,' Hannah agreed. Tears came to her eyes as she gazed at the beautiful portrait.

'Do you want to tell me and your mum about it over tea?' David Moore asked gently. He took his heavy ribbed sweater from the hook on the darkroom door and led them downstairs to the kitchen.

'Mr Winter couldn't find any evidence to show that Sugar and Spice do creep out of Luke's loft to raid food from the shop,' Helen told her mum and dad. She and Hannah had described how the ex-teacher had stomped upstairs to look for clues, then stamped down again in a worse temper than ever. 'He had to admit that he couldn't prove a thing!'

'But we're still worried,' Helen went on. 'He says he's going to ring the pest control officer again tomorrow.'

'Hmm.' Mary Moore cleared away the tea things. 'And you're wondering how anything as beautiful as Sugar and Spice can be thought of as pests?'

Hannah nodded. 'Why can't people just leave them alone?'

Her mum paused at the sink, dishes poised over soapy water. 'I suppose it's because they chew through things you don't want them to, like wires and cables. That can be dangerous. Or because they're renowned for scavenging food wherever they can find it.'

'Scavenging?' Helen echoed with a frown.

'Yes. Squirrels are terrible raiders,' Mary insisted. 'The pickpockets of the animal kingdom!'

'Here comes your lift!' David Moore saw headlights swing from the lane into the farmyard. He interrupted Hannah's next question to warn Mary that it was time to leave for her evening exercise class with Sally Freeman.

She dumped the dishes in the bowl and ran to the mirror to coil her long dark hair on to the top of her head. 'Why not ask Sally about Sugar and Spice while I finish getting ready?' she suggested to Hannah and Helen.

Mrs Freeman was the local vet and a friend of their mother's. She knocked and came into the kitchen wearing a bright striped beret over her short fair hair. Rubbing her hands together and complaining about the cold night, she turfed Speckle out of his favourite spot by the stove.

'What's this about Sugar and Spice?' she asked the twins, having caught the end of Mary's question.

'Sugar and Spice are a pair of squirrels we've been watching. Would *you* say squirrels are pests?' Hannah pounced first.

Sally Freeman blinked and turned down the corners of her mouth. 'Let's see. Well, yes, because they carry fleas, ticks, mites and so on. It's the flea that carries disease; the charming *Orchopeas Howardi*!' She looked more closely at Hannah's unhappy face. 'This wouldn't have anything to do with Mr Winter, would it?'

'How did you know?' Helen jumped at the sound of the old man's name.

'He's already been on the phone to me during evening surgery,' the vet admitted. 'It was squirrel-this and squirrel-that! He wanted my expert opinion on the risks caused by letting them near food. According to Mr Winter, he's "gathering intelligence" for an all-out war on Luke Martin's pair of nesting juveniles!'

Hannah and Helen groaned.

Sally Freeman knitted her brows. 'I have to admit he might have a point,' she said quietly.

'Oh no!' Hannah breathed.

'How come?' Helen asked.

'Well, no animal should be allowed near food, as you know. And if the squirrels were to get into the shop and leave droppings, or if fleas were to hop off their backs on to the cheese or the butter, the spread of bacteria could cause a serious outbreak of food poisoning.' The vet delivered the bad news in a firm, calm voice.

'Is that what you told Mr Winter?' Hannah wanted to know.

Mrs Freeman nodded. 'I was only telling him what he already knew. But I also told him that the pest control people would want more proof that the squirrels can get into Luke's shop. It's a serious matter to bring them in with their rules and regulations, their traps and poison . . .'

Hannah went to look out of the dark window. Helen bit her lip and turned away.

'What did Cecil Winter say to that?' their dad asked.

Sally gave a wry smile. 'You know what he's like. Once he begins this kind of campaign, he doesn't easily give in.' Seeing that Mary was ready to leave, she joined her at the door.

'I suppose he'll tell the whole village?' David guessed what the ex-teacher's tactics would be.

The vet nodded. 'He calls it "looking for allies". We're talking about an all-out war against squirrels here!'

She smiled sympathetically at Helen and Hannah. 'And while I'm giving you the bad news, I'd better warn you that Mr Winter says he's one hundred per cent sure that before the week's out he will have absolute proof that your Sugar and Spice are Doveton's public enemy number one!'

*

Hannah spread the crumpled chocolate wrappings on the bedroom windowsill. 'Here's Mr Winter's proof, if only he knew it!' she said miserably. Guilt gnawed away at her. 'Helen, you don't think we should . . . ?'

'Tell Luke?' Helen shook her head. 'No!'

Their mum was out at her aerobics class, their dad was busy in his attic darkroom.

Hannah picked up one of the scraps of silver paper and examined the sharp teeth marks round the edge. She sighed and turned it this way and that.

'If we let on about this, they'll set traps and poison Sugar and Spice!' Helen cried. 'As it is, the way Mr Winter is carrying on, their days are probably numbered anyway!' She paced up and down the room, trying to come up with a plan of their own.

'You know something?' Hannah held the wrapper up to the light, her face creased into a frown.

'What?' Helen stopped pacing and turned to face Hannah. She could always tell when her twin sister had been struck by an interesting idea.

'I think we were wrong!'

'How?' Helen squinted at the tell-tale wrapper.

'We've been blaming Sugar and Spice for stealing

this chocolate, but take a look at these teeth marks!' Hannah said excitedly. 'See how they've made holes through the middle of the paper? Well, if a squirrel had chewed it, the holes would be different!'

'You mean, not so sharp and pointed?' Helen began to see what she meant. 'Squirrels' front teeth are flat and chisel-shaped, for gnawing through nutshells. But the animal who made these marks has long, pointed teeth!'

'Like a cat,' Hannah whispered. 'Or a fox!'

Helen's eyes glittered. 'Or a dog!' She turned to Hannah.

'Ollie!' they said together.

Mischievous, naughty Ollie, the out-of-control beagle pup!

'Sam was there with him just after we found the first wrappers!' Hannah reminded Helen.

'And he was there again the second time!' Helen added. 'Which means he could well have been sneaking in and chewing the sweets for ages before anyone noticed! Hannah, we've been really stupid not to think of him before now!'

'We just automatically thought it must be Sugar and Spice!'

'And never gave Ollie a thought!'

'When it was staring us in the face all along!' Hannah was thrilled with their discovery.

'But we still don't say anything!' Helen insisted.

'We don't?' Hannah wanted to rush out and tell Mr Winter to stop his campaign against the squirrels.

'No. It wouldn't do any good. What we have to do before we say anything about Ollie is prove that the squirrels can't get out of the loft. That's the only way to ruin Mr Winter's story about them being a health hazard!' Helen got down to serious planning. 'Listen, tomorrow's Tuesday. What we do is call in at Luke's before school.'

Hannah nodded. 'Then what?'

'Remember the box of flour on the landing?'

She nodded again.

Helen went on. 'We ask Luke if we can take a peek at Sugar and Spice. But really, we open one of the bags of flour and lay a trail across the bottom of the door!'

Hannah frowned. 'What for?'

'It's a layer of white powder, right? We make sure it spreads right across. That way, if the squirrels ever try

59

to squeeze under the gap between the door and the floor, they have to tread through the flour. They get it on their feet, right?'

'Right!' Hannah got the idea. 'They would leave a trail of white footprints along the landing!'

'But if they *don't* try to get out of the loft to raid Luke's shop, there'll be no footprints!' Helen spelled it out. 'Simple!'

'Easy-peasy!' Hannah agreed. Like all the best plans, it seemed foolproof.

'Let's go to bed early,' Helen suggested. 'That way, morning will come quicker!'

'Great!' Hannah was half out of her clothes and into her pyjamas. Teeth were brushed, faces washed.

'Night, Dad!' they called up the stairs.

'It's early for bed. Are you ill?' David Moore came down from the attic to say goodnight. 'What are you up to?' he asked when he saw their shiny faces peeping out of the bedclothes.

'Nothing!' they chirped.

'That means something!' He wrinkled his nose, grinned, then turned out the light.

'We're doing something to help Sugar and Spice at

last!' Hannah whispered, as her dad's footsteps shuffled back upstairs to the darkroom.

They cycled down from Home Farm early next morning and stopped at the village shop. Their plan went without a hitch. They laid a trail of flour across the entrance to the loft without Luke suspecting a thing. In fact, he'd been on the phone when they arrived, and beckoned them in without stopping to talk. 'Go on up!' he'd mouthed, guessing that they'd come to see the squirrels. After they'd laid the trail and gone down again, he'd been nowhere to be seen.

'He'll be so pleased when we prove that Sugar and Spice can't get out!' Helen whispered. They'd arrived at school just in time for registration.

'Hazel Greene?' the teacher called.

'Yes, Miss Wesley!'

'Sam Lawson?'

'Yes, Miss!' Sam slid into his seat beside Hannah. He was out of breath from his last-minute dash.

'Hannah Moore?'

'Yes, Miss Wesley!'

'Helen Moore?'

'Yes, Miss Wesley!'

'Guess what?' Sam leaned across as the list of names continued.

'Shh!' Hannah knew that the teacher liked to call the register in silence.

'No, really, you'd better listen to this!' Sam ducked down behind his bag and carried on talking. 'I just called in at Uncle Luke's!'

'So?' Helen leaned across as soon as she heard Luke's name. 'We did too!'

'I know.' Sam peered over the top of his bag at the teacher. 'I bet he didn't tell you the news, did he?'

'What news?' Hannah listened with a sinking feeling. Sam was too nervy; almost gloating at them.

'Something went missing from the shop last night!'

'What?' Helen hissed.

'Three bars of chocolate!' Sam reported. 'And that's not all. Something got inside the cheese counter during the night and nibbled the cheese!'

'No!' Helen refused to believe it.

Sam nodded. 'Guess who's getting the blame?'

Miss Wesley closed the register and frowned across at the whispering in their corner.

Hannah's heart sank into her boots. Someone or something who could get into the shop when the outer door was locked and the shutters were down. Someone or something who liked chocolate and cheese.

Helen answered Sam's question for Hannah. 'Sugar and Spice,' she whispered. Who else would people suspect for the raid on Luke's shop but the star pickpockets of the animal world?

Six

'What will your Uncle Luke do about the things that have gone missing from the shop?' Hannah asked Sam, looking over his shoulder at the work he was doing for the open evening. She was surprised to see that his project had changed. It wasn't on squirrels any more, but on beagles.

'He has to check the shelves to make sure nothing else has been stolen.' Sam wrote a big title: SCENT HOUNDS, and worked on as if nothing had happened.

'Then what?' Helen demanded. It made her cross that Sam didn't seem to care.

' "Scent hounds work in packs . . ." ' Sam read out loud from a library book. He copied the sentence slowly and neatly on to his page.

'Then what will Luke do?' Helen repeated.

'I expect he'll have to ring up about the squirrels,' Sam said in an offhand way. ' "The beagle is a scent hound bred for hare-coursing." ' He read the next sentence and copied it.

'Who will he ring up?' Helen wanted to snatch the paper from Sam and make him concentrate on what she was saying.

'The public health office.' Sam paused and glanced up. 'Uncle Luke says the same as Mr Winter now. If the squirrels can get out of the loft and down into the shop after all, then he'll have to bring in pest control to get rid of them.'

Hannah sat down heavily in her seat. She stared at the unfinished work on squirrels. Their photograph of Sugar and Spice lay on her desk ready for mounting.

Helen leaned closer to Sam and put her hand over his library book.

'Hey!' he protested.

'What if it's *not* Sugar and Spice?' she demanded.

Sam's pale grey eyes flickered. 'What do you mean?'

'What if someone else is stealing the chocolate?' She outstared him with her own blazing brown eyes.

'How can they be?' he scoffed. 'It stands to reason; Uncle Luke's got squirrels in the loft and everyone knows what they're like. They'll squeeze through tiny gaps and eat anything they can get their teeth into.' As he argued, he tried to prise Helen's fingers away from his book.

'That's not real evidence!' Helen insisted. 'That's just guessing.'

'And I suppose you've got a better idea?' Sam finally freed his book and turned the page.

'Maybe.' Helen glanced at Hannah, who nodded. She pointed at the glossy picture of the beagle pup in Sam's book. 'Squirrels aren't the only animals round here that like cheese and chocolate!'

'Meaning what?' Sam blushed and ducked his head behind the book.

'Meaning Ollie!' Helen kept on glaring.

Sam hunched forward. 'You're mad!' he said hotly, snapping the book shut.

From her desk at the front of the classroom, Miss Wesley gave them a warning stare.

'You're saying Ollie's the thief?' Sam demanded.

Helen and Hannah nodded steadily. They could feel Miss Wesley stand up and begin to walk towards them.

'Dream on!' Sam hissed under his breath. Then, with a burst of defiance, he added, 'Prove it!'

Helen glared at him for as long as she dared. 'We will!' she promised, before the teacher told her firmly to sit down and get on with her work.

It seemed that the school would *never* be ready for open evening on time. Pictures were cut and glued, displays mounted on every bit of wall. There was a Herdwick sheep project and a Friesian cow project, a Brown Leghorn hen project and three pieces of work on Border collies. Hamsters, rabbits, parrots and cats were popular too.

'Helen, bring me the stapler, please!' Miss Wesley cried from the top of the stepladder in the entrance hall. Tuesday and Wednesday had sped by. They had half an hour left before the doors opened to the public. 'Hannah, have you got your photograph of the squirrels ready?'

Helen and Hannah's squirrel project was to take

pride of place. The teacher had given it a top grade and decided that it should be the first piece of work that people saw when they walked in through the main entrance.

'How could you help falling in love with these two gorgeous creatures?' Miss Wesley cooed as she stapled the photograph of Sugar and Spice in place and stood back to admire the effect.

And, as they waited that evening in the entrance hall to greet visitors, Helen and Hannah were glad to hear that many people in Doveton agreed.

'Look at those cute little squirrels!' Julie Stott lifted her toddler, Joe, up to the picture. Joe wouldn't be coming to Doveton Junior for a few years yet, but the Stotts believed in finding out all they could about the school.

He gurgled and pointed his chubby finger at the bushy-tailed pair.

'Aren't they the most adorable things?' Valerie Saunders from Doveton Manor stared up at the picture. 'Wouldn't you just love to have them as pets?'

Sally Freeman held her son, Ashley, by the hand. 'Don't let Mr Winter hear you say that!' she warned.

The ex-headteacher had returned to school for the open evening. He strolled down the corridor, hands clasped behind his back, surveying the work displayed on the walls. When he came to Helen and Hannah's section on squirrels, his face creased into a frown.

Slowly he studied the squirrel facts that the twins had gathered. ' "The grey squirrel does not hibernate," ' he read. 'Oh, really?' He turned to the twins with a cool glance, looking for an explanation.

Valerie Saunders and Sally Freeman stayed on. They smiled encouragingly at the twins to give Mr Winter an answer.

'They can't get through the winter without food,' Hannah stammered. 'They need to eat every few days, so they wake up and go to their food store.'

'Harrumph.' The old teacher read on. ' "The upper body is greyish, with a yellowish-brown underside." '

'They're more silvery grey in winter,' Helen explained. 'In summer, they shed their winter coats and they're more brown.'

'Hmm.' Mr Winter rocked backwards and forwards on the balls of his feet. 'Very good. But I see you've omitted a very important section from your project.'

'What would that be, Mr Winter?' Mrs Saunders asked. 'The twins's work seems excellent to me.'

The old man drew himself up to his full height. 'I mean the very obvious health hazard aspect of squirrels,' he insisted.

Helen blushed and bit her lip. Hannah stared blankly at the wall. They knew Mr Winter was about to launch into his favourite subject.

'. . . Quite mistaken to regard these creatures as fluffy pets . . . Spread diseases, damage property, prolific breeders.' He gathered a small audience for his lecture. Valerie Saunders looked worried. Sally Freeman nodded and admitted he was right.

'Wait for it,' Hannah groaned. 'He's going to mention Luke's shop!'

'He'll turn everyone against Sugar and Spice!' Helen muttered. The poor squirrels would be found guilty without trial.

'Squirrels are a major problem!' Mr Winter declared in a loud voice. 'Luckily, some of us are alert to the problem. Why, only this week, I've had cause to contact the public health authorities!'

He gave a blow-by-blow account, and soon the story of the squirrels in Luke Martin's loft spread round the

Sugar and Spice The Pickpockets

school. Julie Stott held Joe close and said she would rather be safe than sorry when it came to making sure he stayed fit and well. Valerie Saunders admitted that cute appearances could be misleading. 'Of course, you can never be too careful where food is concerned,' she confessed.

Guilty! Not even given a chance! Hannah and Helen stood unhappily by the door as the rumours spread.

'What should we do?' Julie asked her husband, Dan. 'Should we stop buying food from the village shop?'

'No need!' Mr Winter interrupted before panic set in. 'I've spoken to Luke today and he agrees with me that the only thing to do is to bring in pest control!'

Hannah sighed. Helen blinked and shuffled her feet. They'd been so busy getting ready for the opening evening that they hadn't had a chance to see Luke since Monday.

'It wouldn't have made any difference,' Hannah whispered, as Mr Winter promised the small knot of listeners that the problem was under control. 'It sounds as if Luke has turned against Sugar and Spice. He wants them out of the loft!'

'But not poisoned!' Helen insisted. She couldn't believe that the shopkeeper could be so ruthless. 'Hannah, we have to talk to him!'

'When?' Hannah put her hands to her ears to block out the sound of Mr Winter's voice. He was describing the common methods of getting rid of pests.

'. . . Similar to Warfarin, the poison used to kill rats . . . Dishes put down by specially trained experts . . . Works within hours once the animal has eaten it.'

'Now!' Helen decided.

They braved the cold, dark October night and ran from the school, along the main street, towards the yellow light of Luke's shop window.

He opened the door to the sound of their knock. 'Hannah – Helen, what are you doing here?' Looking worried and tired, he let them in.

'Is it true?' Hannah demanded, darting into the shop. Her gaze ran along the shelves of cakes and biscuits.

'Have you changed sides? Are you going to poison Sugar and Spice?' Helen came straight to the point.

'Steady on.' The shopkeeper backed off into the storeroom. 'It's not a question of changing sides. But this situation is getting out of hand. Almost every day something else goes missing; last night it was more chocolate. This morning I found a hole in a packet of biscuits!'

'But can you prove it's the squirrels?' Hannah felt sure that Luke would listen to reason.

He sighed. 'The biscuits had teeth marks in them. What more proof do we need?' Shaking his head and shrugging, he told them he was sorry. 'I've got Mr Winter breathing down my neck, as you know.'

Hannah thought fast. 'Last night was Tuesday. And you say there was another raid?'

'And the night before that. Like I said, it's out of hand.'

'OK. So, if we could prove to you that Sugar and Spice couldn't possibly have crept downstairs to steal things from the shop, what would you do then?'

Luke put his head to one side. 'I don't know. I hadn't thought of that.'

Hannah grabbed his sleeve and drew him to the bottom of the stairs. 'The idea is that the squirrels somehow find a way down, right? To do that, they'd have to squeeze through the loft door and along the landing!'

'I suppose so.' Luke was puzzled, but he let himself be led upstairs. 'I hadn't thought of that either.'

Helen followed close behind. 'Wait till you see this!' she promised. She had her fingers crossed tight. This was the moment when Hannah's tricks with the trail of flour had to work!

Hannah reached the landing first. She turned on the light and crept towards the door. Holding her breath, she studied the thin trail of white powder. 'See!' She turned to Helen and Luke in triumph.

Not a single footprint disturbed the thin band of flour across the doorway.

'We put this down on Monday morning!' Helen explained. 'If Sugar and Spice had been creeping out of the loft on all these raids, there would be scuff marks and footprints everywhere!' Her eyes shone, her face broke into a relieved smile.

'They're innocent!' Hannah sighed. 'I knew it all along!'

Seven

'Life isn't that simple!' Luke sat on a cardboard box on the landing, staring at the loft door. 'I wish it was, but it isn't.'

'Why not?' Helen asked. Hadn't they proved that Sugar and Spice couldn't be behind the thefts? 'Why can't you leave them in peace?'

'There are a lot of reasons why not,' Luke sighed. 'First off; Hannah's trick may prove that the squirrels don't come under the door, but there could be other ways they can get into the shop.'

'Such as?' Hannah spoke up. They'd rung for their mum to come and collect them, but meanwhile they tried to persuade Luke that Sugar and Spice weren't the criminals they were made out to be.

'They might get in from the outside.' Luke suggested. 'It's amazing what small gaps they can get through. And the second thing is, the word is out. Everyone in the village knows about the squirrels, thanks to Mr Winter. So I have to be seen to do something about them.'

'What if we tell everyone that Sugar and Spice are innocent?' Helen objected.

'You could try.' Luke looked glum. 'But it still doesn't solve the third problem.'

'What's that?' Hannah's delight was rapidly fading. She had a creepy sensation at the back of her neck, even before Luke gave his answer.

'It's the main reason we can't let the squirrels spend the winter in my nice warm loft,' he said sadly. 'And it comes in the shape of a Mr Frank Watson.'

'Who's he?' Hannah and Helen said together.

Luke sighed and stood up. He went slowly down the stairs without meeting the twins' gaze. 'He's the public health inspector for Nesfield and Doveton. I've already made an appointment to see him. He's coming here at four o'clock tomorrow!'

'All fresh food items to be hygienically wrapped and stored!' Frank Watson stood, pen poised over his red clipboard.

'I keep all the cheeses and butters in the refrigerated unit.' Luke pointed to the spotless glass counter.

'No food to be stored at ground level!' The inspector flicked his stony stare over the shelves.

'Everything fresh is kept behind the counter, for hygiene reasons.' The shopkeeper was nervous as the inspector made a tick in a box and moved on.

Hannah and Helen had run to the shop after school next day. Their hearts had sunk when they'd seen the dark-blue car parked outside. Until that moment, they'd been hoping that Mr Frank Watson wouldn't keep his appointment.

Now they could see he meant business, with his official list, his beady eye and his smart, slicked-back hair.

'Everything seems to be in order down here,' he told Luke. 'Now perhaps you could show me upstairs.'

Hannah watched the man in the grey suit follow Luke through the storeroom. 'I'm going outside. I need some fresh air,' she told Helen.

'I wonder how long they'll be?' Helen chewed her bottom lip. She followed Hannah out on to the pavement and stared up at the almost bare branches of the beech trees.

'Not long.' Out of the corner of her eye, Hannah saw Sam running down the street with Ollie. 'Oh no, not now, please!' she murmured.

The beagle pup came flying towards them. The wind caught his floppy ears as he launched himself at Helen. His white-tipped tail wagged, his pink tongue licked her hands.

'Down, Ollie!' Helen wasn't in the mood to play.

But the puppy didn't understand the command. Again he jumped and wriggled, licked and wagged.

'What's wrong with you two?' Sam caught up at last, and saw their glum faces.

'The health inspector's here,' Hannah told him. 'He's going to look at the loft, then give his verdict on Sugar and Spice.'

'Oh!' Sam sniffed and glanced up at the roof.

Helen wrestled with Ollie. The puppy wouldn't stay

still for a moment. Now he was off to bother Hannah, leaping up again and demanding attention.

'What are you looking at?' Free from Ollie at last, Helen followed Sam's gaze.

'Nothing.' He went to grab his puppy from Hannah, but Ollie slipped away. Sam ran after him round the side of the shop.

But by now, Helen had spotted what had caught Sam's attention. There, sitting on the mossy roof in the very last rays of the autumn sun, were Sugar and Spice.

Spice perched on the ridge, hunching forward over a tasty titbit which he held between both front paws. Sugar saw the twins and froze. Her tail curled over her head, her bright eyes shone.

'Don't move!' Helen breathed, as Hannah too picked out the squirrels on the roof. 'The last thing we want is for them to make a dash inside while the inspector's up there.'

In spite of everything, Hannah couldn't help smiling. 'I'm sure Sugar thinks that if she stays still we won't be able to see her!' The smaller squirrel was like a statue.

Then suddenly, as Ollie came charging back round

the front of Luke's shop, she took fright. With a whisk of her tail and a rapid *tuk-tuk-tuk* she fled across the slates.

Spice dropped his titbit and followed. They reached the edge of the roof together. For a second they paused. Then they flew through the air in soaring jumps, from roof to tree, scrambling along a slender branch, shaking the last leaves to the ground.

'Gone!' Helen sighed. She'd enjoyed their first sight of the squirrels since Sunday.

'Ouch!' Hannah cried. Rough little Ollie had caught her legs as he rushed past. He didn't even stop, but charged on, dodging Sam and galloping up the step into the shop.

'Come back!' Sam was red in the face. He was still too far behind the unruly puppy to grab him.

Ollie ignored him. He yelped with excitement amongst the tempting shelves of cakes and biscuits.

Hannah frowned. 'Mr Watson should see this!' she decided.

Helen nodded. Even if Sam refused to consider Ollie as the sneak chocolate thief, the inspector would have to believe the evidence of his own eyes. 'Let's go and get him!'

They ran quickly into the shop and through the storeroom. Ollie was still causing chaos behind the counter and Sam was trying to rugby-tackle him in a far corner. Taking the steps two at a time, the twins reached the landing at the moment when the inspector and Luke emerged from the loft.

Mr Watson clicked his pen and tucked it in his top pocket. He took off his glasses and folded them. 'Well, there's no sign of the actual squirrels,' he began.

Helen and Hannah stopped in their tracks. The inspector had a quiet, deliberate way of speaking that made you listen, so they pressed themselves against the wall as the two men made their way towards them.

'But of course, they may be sleeping inside the drey,' he went on, frowning at the twins without really noticing them. He was busy thinking. 'In any case, it doesn't really matter. The fact that they've built their nest in the loft gives us enough evidence to act on.'

Luke nodded and led the way downstairs. Hannah and Helen had forgotten all about catching Ollie in the act. Instead, they hung on the inspector's every word.

'I'll have to make a report on what I've seen,' Mr Watson told Luke, who waited for him in the store-room. 'But don't worry, the conditions here are pretty good. I can see that you're not breaking any hygiene regulations.'

'Thanks.' Luke sounded relieved.

'I take it that you ask all customers to leave their pet dogs outside the shop?' The inspector must have heard Ollie bark. He walked through and peered out of the shop door. There on the pavement, the rowdy puppy was still giving Sam the slip.

Luke nodded. He raised his eyebrows at Hannah and Helen. 'Thank heavens Sam managed to keep Ollie outside for a change!' he whispered.

'So!' Frank Watson was out on the pavement now, allowing himself a thin smile at the beagle pup's antics. He turned to Luke. 'Do you want me to give you the unofficial verdict before I go?'

'Yes, please.' Luke followed the inspector into the sun.

Helen and Hannah stood in the doorway, listening to the decision that would seal Sugar and Spice's fate.

'My report will praise the shop for excellent stan-dards of hygiene,' Mr Watson said briskly and brightly.

'No problems at all here, Mr Martin . . . except for the nest in the loft!'

'Yes. What about it?' Luke frowned.

'Quite simple! I'll make my report and tell the pest control people what they're up against; a pair of nesting squirrels on premises where there is fresh food for sale. It's an urgent case, so they'll be here as soon as they can; probably before the weekend.'

'What will they do?' Luke lowered his voice to a whisper. He tried to avoid looking at the twins.

'Simple again!' The businesslike inspector gave what

he thought was a reassuring smile. 'The procedure will be quick and easy. By Monday morning, I think we can safely say that there will be no more squirrels in your loft!'

Eight

Friday dawned grey and misty. Fallen leaves turned soggy underfoot, and fog clung to the branches of the chestnut tree outside Helen and Hannah's bedroom window.

'I'm sorry, girls.' Mary Moore put a breakfast of hot muffins and marmalade on the table. 'This is one of those situations where you have to accept that there's nothing you can do!'

They'd hardly slept for worrying about the squirrels. 'We could ask Luke if we could move the drey!' Hannah suggested. The nest was small enough to pick up and take out of the loft.

Their dad shook his head. 'Then what? Where would you put it?'

'In a tree or a hedge . . . I don't know!' Hannah admitted.

'Look, love; you can't just move a wild animal's winter nest and expect it to take up residence again. The drey would have your scent all over it. There's no way the squirrels would go on using it.'

Hannah poked miserably at her breakfast. Speckle sat quietly at her feet, head resting on his front paws, tail gently wagging. Even he realised something was wrong.

'And it's already very cold at night,' Mary Moore reminded them. 'It's too late for Sugar and Spice to start building a new nest.' She dismissed Hannah's idea once and for all.

'Try not to dwell on it,' David Moore suggested. 'Your mum's right; there's nothing you can do, except carry on as usual.'

Carrying on as usual meant going out to the barn after breakfast to muck out and feed Solo. The grey pony came eagerly to his stall door, snorting and pushing his nose against them. Hannah led him out and began brushing him down, while Helen raked out his bedding. They filled his net with fresh hay and his bucket with clean water. They walked Speckle up the misty fell, then came back and fed him and Socks, the Home Farm cat.

'Hens?' Mary Moore inquired as she dashed through the kitchen in the early morning rush to get to work.

'I've fed them,' Helen said.

'Geese?'

'Done!' Hannah reported.

'Good. Time to get changed for school. I'll see if the car will start. It hates this damp, cold weather.'

For a while, being busy with the morning chores had taken the twins' minds off Sugar and Spice. But once they were ready and sitting in the car as it chugged down the steep hill into the village, the thought of the death sentence hanging over the squirrels hit them again.

'It's not fair!' Helen breathed. She glowered at Mr Winter's house as they passed.

'They're not doing any harm!' Hannah murmured, picturing them snug in their drey, little suspecting what was to come.

'Mum, can you drop us off at the shop?' Helen leaned forward. She could see Carrie Lawson talking to Luke outside, and Sam and Ollie waiting by the Land Rover.

'Only if you promise not to pester Luke about the squirrels,' Mary Moore warned. 'Remember, it's not his fault!'

So they got out of the car with their schoolbags, and endured Ollie's boisterous greeting. They waved their mum goodbye.

As Helen fended off the beagle pup and tried to calm him down, she listened to what Luke's sister had to say.

'And couldn't you ask the pest control people to trap the squirrels?' she asked. 'Poison seems such a cruel way to deal with them.'

'You mean trap them in a cage?' Luke considered the idea. 'Then what?'

'Then they could be kept as pets.' Carrie had her eye on Helen and Hannah. 'I'm sure someone would want to look after them!'

'*We* would!' Hannah didn't hesitate. She gave Mrs Lawson a grateful smile. At last, here was a grown-up who was on their side.

But Luke was already shaking his head. 'I did ask Frank Watson about that. Apparently there's a law that says squirrels can't be kept in captivity without a special licence. And there isn't time to do that here. The only other choice, besides the usual poison, is to kill the squirrels by shooting them.'

Helen gasped. 'Oh no!'

'I agree.' Luke looked pale, as if he hadn't got much sleep either. 'I'm sorry it's come to this,' he told Helen and Hannah.

'All because Mr Winter had it in for the squirrels,' Carrie Lawson murmured. 'If they hadn't attacked his precious Puppy, none of this would have happened.'

'They didn't!' Hannah objected. She'd been there; a witness to prove that Sugar and Spice hadn't even touched the cairn terrier.

'Maybe not. But that's what Mr Winter thinks,' Mrs Lawson pointed out. 'Otherwise, he wouldn't have gone on the warpath and made such a fuss about them being a health hazard. The poor squirrels would probably have been allowed to snooze away the winter in Luke's loft without anyone actually realising they were there!'

Hannah and Helen frowned and stared at Sam Lawson.

'Except for the raids on the chocolate and cheese,'

Luke reminded his sister. 'I'd have been bound to notice that sooner or later. No; to be fair, the squirrels' days were numbered even without Cecil Winter's campaign against them.'

'Assuming it is the squirrels who are sneaking into the shop.' Carrie thrust her hands into the pockets of her green jacket and stamped her feet. She glanced absent-mindedly at Ollie, who had jumped up at the litter bin outside the shop. He poked his nose under the lid and stuck his head right in. Now all that could be seen of him was his hind legs and furiously wagging tail.

'What else could it be? You don't think it could be rats?' Luke's worried frown deepened.

The twins carried on staring at Sam. *Tell them about Ollie! Ollie running riot, Ollie charging between legs and into the shop. Ollie sniffing at the shelves. Ollie's teethmarks on the chocolate wrappers!* They willed him to confess.

But Sam kept his mouth tight shut.

Even when Mr Winter's Puppy came flying down the street, yapping and growling at the sight of the beagle pup, Sam didn't react. It was Helen who stepped across the terrier's path to try and stop him, Hannah who tugged at Ollie's collar to get him out of the litter bin.

'Puppy!' Mr Winter roared from his garden gate. 'Come back here!'

The yapping ball of cream fur flew at the wriggling pup. Puppy launched himself into the attack, teeth bared.

Hannah hung on to Ollie. She felt Puppy's hot breath, saw the angry gleam in his eye.

Ollie squirmed free. He stood his ground. As Puppy's jaws snapped, the beagle bounced at him, paws flashing across the terrier's face. Then there was a flurry of snarls, yaps and squeals.

'Look out!' Mr Winter was trundling down the street in his shirt-sleeves and slippers. 'Stand back!' he ordered as he lunged between the scrapping dogs to part them.

With his hand clutching Puppy's collar, the old man looked up at Carrie Lawson. 'I'm awfully sorry!' he gasped. 'This is most unlike Puppy!'

Mrs Lawson nodded. 'Me too. Ollie is rather a handful, I'm afraid.' She stooped to pick him up.

'Erm, Mr Winter, look at Puppy's nose.' Helen had spotted a fresh cut, almost the same as the one Puppy had had the Saturday before. It was a tiny, red mark on his hairy nose, made by a swipe from Ollie's paw.

The ex-headteacher took out his handkerchief and dabbed at the cut. 'You see, Puppy!' he scolded. 'This is what happens when you disobey orders!'

For a few moments, Hannah couldn't believe her ears. Mr Winter was saying sorry and telling precious Puppy off! But then, he could hardly deny what he'd seen with his own eyes.

'Now you'll have another nasty scar!' He stopped dabbing and set the terrier back on his feet. 'That's odd!'

'What is?' Luke crouched to examine the damage to Puppy's nose.

'This cut; it's identical!' Mr Winter glanced up at Ollie wriggling in Carrie Lawson's arms. He turned to quiz Sam. 'Were you here with your puppy last Saturday afternoon?'

Helen and Hannah watched Sam shuffle and twitch. He backed off, bumped into the litter bin, turned this way and that.

'Come on, Sam. Tell Mr Winter what he wants to know.' Carrie Lawson gave him a small shove forward. 'You were here at Luke's, weren't you?'

'Yes,' Sam admitted in a croaky voice.

'And did you see Puppy and Ollie fighting then?' The truth began to dawn on the old man's face. His bushy eyebrows shot up, his eyes opened wide.

'Yes.'

'You mean . . . the cut . . . the scar on Puppy's nose . . . ?' For once, Mr Winter was lost for words.

'Yes,' Sam muttered. He shuffled again and took a deep breath. 'OK, it's true!' he confessed. 'Ollie did scratch Puppy's nose!'

'And you let the squirrels take the blame?' Luke cut in.

Sam nodded and blushed scarlet.

'*Hmph!*' Mr Winter shot glances from Puppy to Ollie, and from Sam to the twins.

'What else?' Mrs Lawson prompted, guessing that her son had more to say.

'That's not all I let Sugar and Spice take the blame for.' The words rushed out of Sam's mouth now. 'I was scared Ollie would get into bad trouble if I owned up. I mean, he's only a little pup; he doesn't realise what he's doing is wrong!'

'Slow down, Sam.' Luke took him by the shoulder. 'What is it that you didn't dare own up to?'

95

'He's always hungry, see! Mum can tell you; he eats everything in sight!'

'It's true.' Carrie Lawson kept a tight hold of Ollie while Sam got everything off his chest.

'And Hannah and Helen kind of made it worse!' he gabbled on. 'They knew that it was Ollie and not the squirrels. That meant I had to cover up for him even more!'

'Whoa!' Luke said again. He turned to the twins. 'What is he trying to tell us?'

Helen drew a deep breath. The facts had tumbled out. Now she had to put them into plain English. 'Sugar and Spice didn't raid your shop.'

'Ollie did.' Hannah gazed up at Luke's mossy roof. The truth was out at last. Too late to save the squirrels, but now at least everyone knew who the real thief was.

Nine

Carrie Lawson told the twins how sorry she was. She said she realised they must be upset. 'I saw your project displayed on the wall on open evening,' she murmured. 'It was obvious you really loved your subject.'

'I'm sorry too.' Sam hung his head.

'That's OK. We know you were only trying to cover up for Ollie.' Hannah could hardly blame him for not owning up sooner. After all, Sam loved his puppy too.

'We guessed the truth because of the toothmarks,' Helen explained to Luke and Mr Winter. She found it harder than Hannah to make excuses for Sam. 'We found some chocolate wrappings that had been chewed up. The teeth were the wrong shape for squirrels.'

'And why didn't you reveal your findings to us?' Mr Winter tutted and frowned. 'After all, we're reasonable people; not prone to passing hasty judgments. We would have given full consideration to your point of view!'

Neither Hannah nor Helen could think of anything to say. 'Reasonable' was not a word they would have used about Mr Winter. He was a steam-roller who squashed you flat.

'I wouldn't let them,' Sam confessed. 'It's all my fault.'

'Whoever is to blame, it doesn't alter the fact that the pest control person is due here at four o'clock this afternoon.' Luke shook his head and looked at his watch. 'And if you three don't get a move on, you're going to be late for school!'

It was time to split up. Mr Winter retreated thoughtfully to his terraced house with a subdued Puppy. Carrie Lawson put Ollie into the Land Rover and promised Luke that she would keep a closer eye on him in future. Sam trudged shame-faced to school with Hannah and Helen. They stopped in the main entrance, under the portrait of Sugar and Spice.

The two squirrels stared into the camera. Every whisker, every silky hair in their long, bushy tails was in focus. They looked so alive you almost expected them to leap out of the photograph on one of their swift, acrobatic runs.

Sam sighed.

'Don't say it!' Helen whispered. She couldn't take her eyes off the portrait as the bell went for registration and crowds of children hurried past.

'No. Don't say anything,' Hannah agreed. She found it hard to believe that Sugar and Spice only had hours to live.

'But I am. I'm sorry!' Sam blurted out. 'I never wanted it to end like this!'

A plain white van drew up outside the village shop. A woman in a navy blue jumper and trousers got out. It was exactly four o'clock.

Hannah and Helen had been drawn to the spot after school. Sam had asked if he could come with them, so they'd arrived together, just as Mr Winter marched down the street.

I thought I'd better keep an eye on things,' he explained. 'We wouldn't want anything to go wrong at this stage, would we?'

Yes! Hannah thought.

We would! Helen had her last hopes pinned on the pest control van not arriving as planned.

But here it was. And the woman in the uniform was opening the back doors and taking out a large hold-all. She looked up and down the street, then checked the address on her list. With a brief nod, she walked into the shop.

'Come along,' Mr Winter said briskly. 'Helen and Hannah, since you're here, you can make yourselves useful!'

They obeyed without thinking, following the old man in a daze.

'Good afternoon, I'm Cecil Winter. I spoke to you on the telephone.' He introduced himself to the council official, who was busy talking to Luke.

'Ah yes, Mr Winter. I remember.' The woman turned her head with an irritated frown. She saw Helen, Hannah and Sam hovering behind him.

'I represent the villagers who are concerned about the squirrels,' he went on, pompously brushing aside the woman's frosty reaction. 'We're worried about the possible health risk, because of course squirrels should not be regarded as harmless, pretty creatures, but as a definite source of food poisoning!'

The woman gave him a faint, empty smile, then turned her back. 'Where exactly have they made their drey?' she asked Luke.

Mr Winter bustled forward. 'Now, that's why I've brought these girls along! They're the ones who can locate the very spot in the loft!'

Inwardly Helen groaned. Hannah backed towards the door.

'Very well. Just wait a little while until I've finished explaining things to Mr Martin.' The pest control officer took Mr Winter at his word and accepted the offer of help. She reassured Luke that no one need know that she'd been. 'We're very discreet,' she told him. 'People can sometimes be a bit funny about our visits. That's why we travel in plain vans.'

Luke looked tense. 'That's OK. Just tell me what to expect from here on in.'

The woman tapped her bag. 'The poison is in here. I assess the situation and lay it in small dishes where the squirrels are most likely to come across it. Oh, by the way, you don't have any pets in the house, do you? There's a substance mixed in with the poison that makes all animals want to take a nibble at it!'

He shook his head. 'No. And I'll make sure my visitors don't bring any until this business is over and done with.' He gave Sam a meaningful glance.

'What about the doves? They often fly on to the roof.' Hannah reminded him that the poison would harm the white birds if they pecked at it by mistake.

'They don't come inside, do they?' The woman from the council didn't think they should worry about the doves. She was ready to begin. 'This chemical works extremely fast,' she assured everyone. 'It's highly dangerous, but effective. Once I site the dishes, the job is usually over in a day or so. I'll come back on Monday to remove them. After that you should have no more trouble.'

She meant well with her brisk, breezy manner, but every word she spoke hammered at Hannah and

Helen's hearts. They showed her upstairs and along the landing like convicts going to the gallows.

The woman ducked her head as she stepped through the low door into the loft. She clicked on a torch and shone its bright beam round the dusty space.

The beam caught the broken mirror and flashed a reflection. Hannah and Helen saw themselves, pale-faced and trembling, standing behind the pest control officer. Then she swept the beam on, across the old trunks and packing-cases, over the heavy roof-beams, until it rested in the far corner of the room.

'There!' The woman recognised the rough, round drey. She turned to Hannah. 'Would you hold the torch steady for me while I get what I need out of my bag?'

Hannah took the torch and kept it aimed at the drey. But her hand wasn't steady. The beam shook and slid away from the target.

'Steady on, there!' Mr Winter instructed from outside the loft. He bent to peer through the door. 'Let the lady see what she's doing!'

Helen could make out three small, square plastic dishes. The woman had laid them on the floor and

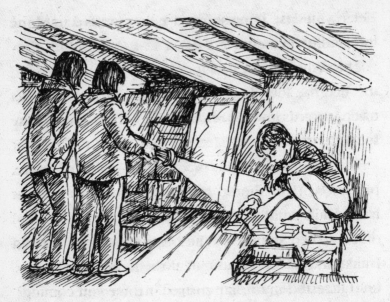

filled them with green pellets. Now she was deciding where to leave them.

'One here, by the door,' she decided. 'One under the eaves.' She crouched and crawled forward between the cases until she could reach the angle where the roof met the floor. This was where she laid the second dish.

'And one on the packing-case under the drey!' Carefully she carried the third dish towards Sugar and Spice's winter nest.

Hannah's hand shook badly now. She half expected the squirrels to smell the bait and peek out of the drey.

They would be hungry. Even if they waited until the loft was quiet again, it couldn't be long before they gobbled the poison down.

'OK, that's it.' The young woman picked her way back towards the door. Dusting herself down, she took the torch from Hannah and went looking for Luke. 'Mr Martin, could you sign this form for me, please. It states the time that I arrived; just for our records, if you don't mind . . .'

Her voice trailed off along the landing, leaving Helen and Hannah standing alone in the loft.

'Hannah? Helen?' Sam peered in. 'Are you coming?'

'Soon.' Helen cleared her throat to answer. 'Tell me this is a bad dream!' she whispered to Hannah.

Miserably Hannah shook her head. 'It's really happening.' This was goodbye to Sugar and Spice.

They stood in silence. Overhead, they heard Luke's doves coo and call.

'Do you think they're asleep?' Helen murmured. There was no sound from the drey; no rustling of dry leaves or faint *wrruhh-wrruhh* from the squirrels as they waited for the intruders to depart.

'Probably.' Hannah couldn't resist creeping forward for one last look. She stepped over the old roller-blind, past the broken mirror, finding her way in the gloom.

'Mind the dish!' Helen warned. She followed close behind, pointing to the shallow tray by the packing-case.

Hannah listened again. 'You'd think they'd be awake!' she said, puzzled. 'Surely they've heard us by now!'

'But you know what they do when they're scared,' Helen whispered. 'They freeze until the danger's passed.'

Hannah peered at the drey. Close to, she could see how untidy it was. The rough bundle of twigs and leaves was practically falling apart. 'When did we last see Sugar and Spice in here?' she asked Helen.

'Sunday; when I took the photograph. Why?'

'But we did see them outside, didn't we?' Hannah was thinking fast.

'Once. Up on the roof.' Helen moved in for an even closer look. 'You'd expect to hear something!' she said. A *tuk-tuk* warning from inside the nest, a moaning or a clattering of teeth.

'Don't touch!' Hannah warned. She gasped as Helen leaned against the packing-case and stood on tip-toe.

The nest wobbled. A twig broke loose and fell.

Still nothing from inside.

Hannah craned her neck to see inside. 'Here's the entrance!' She found a gap. Through a crack of light in the slate roof, she could see a lining of brown leaves and dry grass.

Helen leaned forward again. Another section of the drey shook and fell off. Twigs scattered across the top of the case. 'Aren't they in there?' she breathed.

Messy leaves were stuffed into the bottom of the drey, sharp twigs poked inwards. 'It's not even finished!' Hannah said. She turned to Helen.

'Empty?' Helen whispered.

Hannah nodded. 'Sugar and Spice don't live here after all!'

Ten

'Perhaps it was your camera flash that scared them off!' David Moore stood outside Luke's shop, listening to the twins' gabbled news. 'It occurred to me at the time that they might not be very happy to suddenly find themselves in the middle of all that media attention!'

He'd driven down from Home Farm to see if Helen and Hannah wanted a lift home from school. When he'd missed them there, he'd guessed where they would be and followed them down the High Street.

'But it's fantastic, Dad!' Helen fizzed with

excitement. 'There was no food inside the drey, and the twigs and leaves were all higgledy-piggledy!'

'Sugar and Spice have abandoned the nest!' Hannah spoke with a satisfied sigh. 'Who would have thought of that?' She felt the knot of worry in her stomach loosen.

'So where did they go instead?' David Moore scratched his head and looked up to the roof.

Meanwhile, Luke and Sam stepped out on to the road to see if they could stop the pest control officer and pass on the good news. But it was too late; her van was disappearing round the bend as Carrie Lawson's Land Rover came into view.

'Of course, the key to avoiding these bungles is to check and double check your facts before you contact the authorities!' Mr Winter was speaking to no one in particular. He rocked back on his heels, hands clasped behind his back, and lamented the waste of public money. 'Consider the cost!' he went on. 'There's the wages of the officials involved, for a start! All because someone supposed, wrongly as it turns out, that the drey was inhabited!'

Helen could hardly believe her ears. Wasn't Mr Winter the one who'd failed to check his facts? But she was too happy to care. Sugar and Spice had fled the loft. The dreadful poison would lie useless on the floor.

As Mrs Lawson's car pulled up by the kerb and Ollie leaped out, Hannah went to stroke him. 'Did you hear that, Ollie? Sugar and Spice are safe!'

The little beagle jumped up and waggled his backside. He yapped and licked her hands. Then, when he spotted two doves flutter from the roof up into the high branches of the beech tree, he flung himself at the base of the smooth trunk and barked himself into a frenzy.

The doves looked coolly down. They fanned their tails and cooed.

'What I propose to do now is to ring the central public health office in Nesfield!' Mr Winter set course for his own house. 'I shall tell them the latest developments. Hopefully, they will contact their officer by mobile telephone and she will return forthwith!'

Luke smiled at the twins as the old man sailed off down the street. 'Uh-oh, watch out!' he hissed.

Ollie had grown bored with the doves, turned tail and made a mad dash for the shop.

Carrie Lawson tried to stop him. Ollie swerved and

ran on. He was up the step, ears flapping, the white tip of his tail bobbing, before anyone had time to think.

Helen and Hannah moved first. They heard the others follow, but they were on the puppy's tail, chasing him through the shop as he bounced up at the glass-fronted counter and snaffled the nearest chocolate bar.

'Did you *see* that!' Hannah cried.

Ollie made a dive for the storeroom, his jaws clenched around a bar of fruit and nut.

Helen scooted after him. She made a grab for him at the bottom of the stairs, missed and fell flat.

Hannah jumped over her and chased the puppy up the stairs. 'Come back!'

'He's heading for the loft!' Helen called to the others as she picked herself up. *The loft!* Suddenly she gasped.

'The door's still open!' Hannah yelled. She could hear Ollie's footsteps charging along the landing as she took the stairs two at a time.

'Oh no!' Sam wailed from the bottom of the stairs. 'He'll eat the poison!'

Not if we can help it! Helen thought. She flew upstairs after Hannah and Ollie.

The puppy bounded towards the loft. He stopped at the open door to sink his sharp canine teeth into the silver wrapper. He shook the chocolate free. It was gone in a flash.

'Here, Ollie!' Hannah knelt on the floor and reached out her hand.

A lick of the lips with his pink tongue, then Ollie was nose to the floor, snuffling over the threshold into the loft.

'No; come back!' Helen knew there was a dish of poison inside the door. Ollie was a scent hound; he must have smelled it by now!

One mouthful of the green pellets and he would be a goner! Hannah crawled gingerly towards him. 'Here, boy; please!'

The puppy looked back and tossed his head. He went on regardless.

The only thing to do was to sprint for it. Helen made a mad dash; along the landing, through the door, keeping her eye on the white tip of his wagging tail.

She pounced. Just as Ollie's sharp nose had located the first dish of poison, Helen fell on top of him. She put her arms around his middle and tackled him sideways to safety.

Ollie yelped and struggled. His legs whirled like windmills, his tail battered against Helen's cheek. But she kept firm hold.

'Well done!' Hannah dragged Helen to her feet, pulled her and Ollie through the door on to the landing, and slammed the door shut. 'It's OK, he didn't touch a single pellet!' she called down the stairs.

'You saved him!' Sam reached the top first, followed by Luke, Carrie and David Moore. He dashed to take his naughty puppy from a dazed Helen and take him downstairs.

'I'm sorry,' Carrie told Luke. 'I promise, that's the very last time I bring Ollie anywhere near the shop!'

'At least until he's trained,' Luke sighed.

Ollie must have heard them passing sentence. No more delicious chocolate from the sweet counter! He yelped and whined as Sam took him to the car.

They trooped out to watch the puppy locked safely inside the Land Rover. Carrie dipped into her purse to fork out for all the stolen chocolate bars sneaked by the little pickpocket. 'It's the least I can do,' she told Luke with a rueful smile.

'Those doves . . .' Hannah sighed, as Helen rubbed dust from her knees and elbows. She gazed up at the tall beech trees.

'What about them?' All Helen knew was that they'd set Ollie off before he'd charged into the shop.

'. . . What are they doing up there?' Hannah cocked her head to one side.

'Sitting. Cooing. Doing what doves do.' What now? Helen shot a glance at her sister.

'But why are they in the tree? Why aren't they on the dovecote?' Hannah noticed that all the doves had gathered in the branches, and this was unusual.

'I don't know. Do you want me to climb up and ask them?'

'I mean, I haven't actually seen them where they should be, on the roof of their own house, for ages. Since last weekend . . . !' She tailed off.

Together Hannah and Helen let their gaze drift down from the doves in the trees to the round wooden dovecote. It stood on a tall pole about six metres above the ground, close to the side wall of Luke's shop. Normally the birds would come and go through a row of tiny arched openings round the circumference.

As the twins stared and the doves cooed down from the high branches, a silvery grey head popped out of one of the doorways. The head had huge, dark eyes, pointed ears and long whiskers.

'Spice!' Hannah whispered.

Then another head popped out of the next door-way. The nose wrinkled, the ears twitched.

'Sugar!' Helen sighed.

Sam and Carrie, Luke and David Moore came to stare.

The squirrels looked down at their audience. Out came their heads, then in, then out again, like cuckoos

in a cuckoo clock. At last, brave Spice emerged on to
the white roof. He scrambled up and leaped for the
nearest tree.

'*Chuck-char, chuck-charee*!' he called to Sugar.

She followed nimbly, scurrying along the branch
after him, clutching the silver-grey trunk, trailing her
long, bushy tail after her.

Then Spice launched out along another branch,
swinging upside-down, regaining his footing, scam-
pering on.

'He's showing off!' Hannah smiled. She tilted her
head back to see the squirrels' antics.

Sugar leaped to a lower level, nipped a couple of leaves from a twig with her sharp front teeth, held them there and bounded back to the trunk. She reappeared, ready to make a leap back to the dovecote.

But Spice wanted to thrill his audience for a few seconds more. He reached the end of his branch and teetered there. The slender branch swayed and dipped. Spice clung on, plucked a nut from a twig, sat back, then jumped.

'Oh!' Helen covered her eyes and peeped through a gap in her fingers.

The squirrel soared through the air. Down he plummeted . . . and landed beside Sugar on the white wooden roof.

'Oh!' Helen cried again, this time with relief.

They watched the two tails twirl and whisk as the squirrels lowered themselves towards the arched doorways. They popped their heads inside, looked back once, then were gone.

'What were the leaves for?' Sam gasped.

'To line their nest!' Hannah whispered.

'And the nuts are for their food store!' Helen sighed.

'That's where they moved on to!' Luke said with a laugh. 'The little rascals have turned the doves out of their house and squatted in the dovecote!'

The homeless doves flew down from the trees to the roof of the shop. They puffed out their chests and cooed quietly.

'It looks like a job for you, David!' Luke said.

'Yes, Dad, you're good at woodwork!' Helen cried.

'It's the weekend. We'll help!' Hannah offered.

'Help me do what?' Their dad backed off towards the car.

'Build a new home for the doves!' Helen and Hannah said together.

'We'll need wood and nails and white paint.' Hannah began to plan ahead.

'And a couple of spare days!' David Moore joked.

'Oh, Da-ad!' Hannah pleaded. 'We can't turf Sugar and Spice out of their new home; not after what they've been through!' She glanced back at the dovecote, hoping for one more glimpse of the contented pair.

'We could build it ourselves!' Helen suggested brightly. She gave Hannah a secret grin.

'Oh no! Definitely not that!' Their dad gave in, as she had known he would. 'I'll build it. It needs an expert. You stand by and hand me the nails.'

So that was that. Sam and Carrie joined Ollie in the Land Rover and drove off to Crackpot Farm. The puppy bounced up at the back window and barked his head off.

Luke stood on the doorstep smiling at the twins and David Moore as they worked out detailed plans for the new dovecote. 'I'll keep an eye on Sugar and Spice for you!' he promised.

And Helen and Hannah got into the car at last. They leaned out of the window as their dad set off for Home Farm, still hoping for another glance of the new couple setting up home in the old dove-cote.

'There!' Helen whispered, as they pulled away from the kerb.

Two heads popped out. Two quick twists and twirls, and the squirrels were on the roof, tails curled over their heads, clutching beech nuts and nibbling supper in the long afternoon shadows.

Jenny Oldfield

'A luxury home for two!' Hannah sighed.

The twins settled back in the car for the journey home, and pictured a warm, safe winter for Sugar and Spice after all.

SOPHIE THE SHOW-OFF
Home Farm Twins 15

Jenny Oldfield

Meet Helen and Hannah. They're identical twins – and mad about the animals on their Lake District farm!

Sophie's a rescue cat with a habit of showing off – and it's causing all sorts of problems! Parading by the lake in front of tourists, she slips off the ferry rail; stalking doves on the shop roof, she nearly takes a tumble. Luckily for her, the twins are on hand to help. But now Sophie plans to put in an appearance at the local cricket match! Can Helen and Hannah stop her?

h HODDER

Another Hodder Children's book

*Look out for the Home Farm Twins
Summer Special – coming soon!*

STANLEY THE TROUBLEMAKER

Jenny Oldfield

*Meet Helen and Hannah. They're identical
twins – and mad about the animals on their
Lake District farm!*

Stanley's a champion hamster, and he's favourite to win the Doveton Summer Show.
But behind the scenes, rival owners are plotting, and when Stanley escapes from his cage
just before judging begins, Helen and Hannah
suspect someone's let him out on purpose.
The twins vow to find him – but Stanley's not
so keen to be found . . .

HOME FARM TWINS
Jenny Oldfield

66127 5	Speckle The Stray	£3.50	☐
66128 3	Sinbad The Runaway	£3.50	☐
66129 1	Solo The Homeless	£3.50	☐
66130 5	Susie The Orphan	£3.50	☐
66131 3	Spike The Tramp	£3.50	☐
66132 1	Snip and Snap The Truants	£3.50	☐
68990 0	Sunny The Hero	£3.50	☐
68991 9	Socks The Survivor	£3.50	☐
68992 7	Stevie The Rebel	£3.50	☐
68993 5	Samson The Giant	£3.50	☐
69983 3	Sultan The Patient	£3.50	☐
69984 1	Sorrel The Substitute	£3.50	☐
69985 X	Skye The Champion	£3.50	☐
70399 7	Scruffy The Scamp	£3.50	☐

All Hodder Children's books are available at your local bookshop or newsagent, or can be ordered direct from the publisher. Just tick the titles you want and fill in the form below. Prices and availability subject to change without notice.

Hodder Children's Books, Cash Sales Department, Bookpoint, 39 Milton Park, Abingdon, OXON, OX14 4TD, UK. If you have a credit card you may order by telephone – (01235) 831700.

Please enclose a cheque or postal order made payable to Bookpoint Ltd to the value of the cover price and allow the following for postage and packing:
UK & BFPO – £1.00 for the first book, 50p for the second book, and 30p for each additional book ordered up to a maximum charge of £3.00.
OVERSEAS & EIRE – £2.00 for the first book, £1.00 for the second book, and 50p for each additional book.

Name ....

Address ....

....

....

If you would prefer to pay by credit card, please complete:
Please debit my Visa/Access/Diner's Card/American Express (delete as applicable) card no:

Signature ....

Expiry Date ....

ANIMAL ALERT SERIES
Jenny Oldfield

All Hodder Children's books are available at your local bookshop or newsagent, or can be ordered direct from the publisher. Just tick the titles you want and fill in the form below. Prices and availability subject to change without notice.

Hodder Children's Books, Cash Sales Department, Bookpoint, 39 Milton Park, Abingdon, OXON, OX14 4TD, UK. If you have a credit card you may order by telephone – (01235) 831700.

Please enclose a cheque or postal order made payable to Bookpoint Ltd to the value of the cover price and allow the following for postage and packing:
UK & BFPO – £1.00 for the first book, 50p for the second book, and 30p for each additional book ordered up to a maximum charge of £3.00.
OVERSEAS & EIRE – £2.00 for the first book, £1.00 for the second book, and 50p for each additional book.

Name . . . .

Address . . . .

. . . .

. . . .

If you would prefer to pay by credit card, please complete:
Please debit my Visa/Access/Diner's Card/American Express (delete as applicable) card no:

Signature . . . .

Expiry Date . . . .